Daniel Treherne

Stephen The Spider

Bumblebee Books
London

BUMBLEBEE PAPERBACK EDITION

Copyright © Daniel Treherne 2022

The right of Daniel Treherne to be identified as author of
this work has been asserted in accordance with sections 77 and 78 of the Copyright,
Designs and Patents Act 1988.

A CIP catalogue record for this title is
available from the British Library.

ISBN: 978-1-83934-605-7

Bumblebee Books is an imprint of
Olympia Publishers.

First Published in 2022

Bumblebee Books
Tallis House
2 Tallis Street
London
EC4Y 0AB

Printed in Great Britain

www.olympiapublishers.com

Dedication

I dedicate this book to my wonderful grandchildren for giving me the inspiration to write these stories.

Stephen the spider was hiding under the bed. He was very hungry because this morning he was running away from a man with a slipper that was trying to hit him.

Stephen ran into a chair leg and broke all of his teeth and now he couldn't eat. Stephen used to eat the biscuit crumbs which Eres used to drop on the floor but now he couldn't bite them.

Eres's dad didn't like spiders so if he saw one he would try and hit it. Don't know why, spiders can't hurt you.

Stephen was very hungry and had tummy pains because he hadn't eaten for a very long time. Stephen heard Eres coming up the stairs with her milk and cookies. Stephen was waiting for Eres to drop some crumbs, when she did, Stephen ran over to grab a big crumb.

Eres saw Stephen. "Are you hungry?" said Eres.

"I am," said Stephen, "but I can't eat these big crumbs." Then he told Eres what happened to his teeth.

Eres had an idea. "I will make these crumbs small for you," and she put her glass of milk on top of the crumbs and pressed down really hard. It worked, she then saw Stephen climb up the wall and on to the bedside cabinet and start eating the very small crumbs.

Stephen ate all of the biscuit crumbs really quickly. When he finished he felt full, he said thank you to Eres and Eres said she will do the same tomorrow.

Stephen was really happy that he had found a friend to help him.

Eres was downstairs watching television when she heard a lot of banging and running going on upstairs.

She went running upstairs to see what was going on and she could see her dad banging on the carpet with his slipper. "What are you doing, Dad?" said Eres.

"Trying to get this spider," said Eres's dad.

"Don't!" shouted Eres. "He's my friend."

"Too late," said Eres's dad, "I've got him."

Eres was really upset and started to cry a lot. Eres's mum cuddled Eres and told her not to cry. "But he was my friend and his name was Stephen," said Eres.

Eres cried for a long time, she was not happy. "Why did Dad have to hit my friend? He did nothing wrong."

It was bedtime and Eres's mum said, "Go and get ready for bed and I will bring your milk and cookies up to bed for you." Eres got ready for bed and was really upset, she was sat in her bed when her mum brought up her milk and cookies.

Eres was drinking her milk and cookies and feeling very sad about Stephen when she saw something move under the wardrobe. She got out of bed to see what it was. As she bent down she could see a spider, the spider saw Eres and gave her a big smile. As soon as Eres saw the spider smile she knew it was Stephen because he had no teeth. Eres had a smile as big as Stephen's.

Eres put her hand out and Stephen limped on to it, she carried Stephen to the bedside cabinet. Stephen told Eres that the slipper had only hit his leg and then he ran under the floorboards and stayed there until it was safe to go to Eres's bedroom.

Eres put the glass on top of the cookie crumbs and pushed hard then Stephen ate all the cookie crumbs.

Stephen didn't go out of Eres's bedroom again, he stayed there and every night he would come out for cookies and have a chat with Eres.

About the Author

This is Daniel's first children's book to be published. As a musician he is used to writing lyrics for songs and then books. The writing started as a hobby but grew into a passion. Daniel has been married to Tracey for thirty-nine years. They have three children and four grandchildren which give Daniel the inspiration to write these stories.

Acknowledgements

Thank you for my family and friends
for their support and encouragement.

Printed in Great Britain
by Amazon

83377664R00016